Portage Public Library $11.90

Sunflowers

This book has been reviewed
for accuracy by
Jerry Doll
Professor of Agronomy
University of Wisconsin—Madison.

Library of Congress Cataloging in Publication Data

Pohl, Kathleen.
   Sunflowers.

   (Nature close-ups)
   Adaptation of: Himawari / Oda Hidetomo.
   Summary: A detailed look at the life cycle of
the sunflower.
   1. Sunflowers—Juvenile literature. [1. Sunflowers]
I. Oda, Hidetomo. Himawari. II. Title. III. Series.
QK495.C74P55   1986   583'.55   86-26228
   ISBN 0-8172-2710-5 (lib. bdg.)
   ISBN 0-8172-2728-8 (softcover)

This edition first published in 1987 by Raintree Publishers

Text copyright © 1987 by Raintree Publishers Limited Partnership,
translated from *Sunflowers* copyright © 1980 by Hidetomo Oda.

Photographs copyright © 1980 by Hidekazu Kubo.

World English translation rights for *Color Photo Books on Nature*
arranged with Kaisei-Sha through Japan Foreign-Rights Center.

All rights reserved. No part of this book may be reproduced or utilized
in any form or by any means, electronic or mechanical, including
photocopying, recording, or by any information storage and retrieval
system, without permission in writing from the Publisher. Inquiries
should be addressed to Raintree Publishers, 310 W. Wisconsin Avenue,
Milwaukee, Wisconsin 53203.

3 4 5 6 7 8 9 10   99 98 97 96 95 94 93 92 91 90

Sunflowers

Adapted by
Kathleen Pohl

Raintree Publishers
Milwaukee

◀ **Sunflower seeds.**

The sunflower seed is protected inside a hard shell. Some people crack the shells open to eat the seeds. Others eat the shells, as well.

▶ **A seed taking root.**

Sunflower seeds are planted in the spring of the year. If growing conditions are right—with good soil, enough rainfall, and plenty of sunlight—the seed will soon begin to sprout, or germinate. The white sprout becomes the root of the new plant.

If you have ever seen a field of tall yellow sunflowers nodding in the wind, you know how colorful they are. Each giant flower head is framed with bright yellow petals, like the rays of the sun. That is how the sunflower gets its name.

Sunflowers are native to America. Early American Indians used the seeds for food and for cooking oil. The seeds were ground into flour, which was made into bread and cakes. The shells were roasted and ground up to made a drink that tasted much like coffee. Cough syrups and other medicines were made from sunflower seeds.

Today, sunflowers are raised by farmers for a variety of reasons. The seeds are sold as birdseed, and as chicken and cattle feed. They are also commonly marketed as a health food for people. Russia is the country that grows the most sunflowers for commercial purposes. The Russians eat sunflower seeds the way Americans eat peanuts. And the country gets 90 percent of all its vegetable oil from sunflower seeds.

A seed sprouting.

Root hairs forming.

◀ **A seed germinating.**

Moisture in the soil softens the hard shell that protects the seed. As the seed absorbs water, it expands and breaks through the shell. It forms a root, with many tiny root hairs. These reach out to absorb water and nutrients from the soil.

The sunflower root reaches far down into the ground. Seed leaves emerge and begin to grow up through the soil.

▲ Seed leaves pushing above the ground.

The seed leaves have broken out of the shell and pushed their way out of the earth. If there is plenty of sunshine, they will soon turn a darker green and begin to grow larger.

A few days after sunflower seeds are planted in the spring, many of them will sprout and take root. The young root pushes deeper and deeper into the soil. Soon it develops fine root hairs that reach out into the soil to absorb water and nutrients for the growing plant. Secondary, or lateral, roots begin to branch off from the main root.

As the young roots grow downward, tiny leaves begin to push their way up through the soil. These are called seed leaves because they actually formed inside the seed coat. The seed leaves contain stored nutrients that are necessary for the young plant's growth.

◀ A young sunflower root.

The plant root has several functions. It supports the plant stem. And it absorbs water and minerals from the soil for the growing plant. The left photo shows the main root (yellow arrow) and lateral roots (pink arrow). The right photo shows many tiny root hairs on the sides of the root.

▼ **A bud growing between the seed leaves.** The plant's main stem and leaves will develop from the bud that appears between the seed leaves.

▲ **The true leaves form.**

A pair of true leaves has formed between the seed leaves on this sunflower plant.

▲ **The leaves grow rapidly.**

As new buds form along the stem, new leaves grow there.

Before long, true leaves begin to grow between the seed leaves. As the nutrition in the seed leaves is used up, they drop off. The true leaves take over the job of providing food for the growing plant. It is in the green leaves of sunflower plants, as in other plants, that food is produced. The complex process by which plants make food is called photosynthesis. Photosynthesis means "to produce with light."

In order for photosynthesis to take place, the plant leaves must absorb sunlight. The sunflower leaves combine energy from the sun with carbon dioxide and water to produce food. Sunflower leaves grow in such a way that each leaf is able to catch as much sunlight as possible. The leaves grow in pairs. Each pair grows at right angles to the pair below and above it on the sunflower stalk.

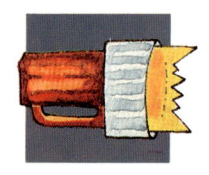

● **Some insects feed on sunflower leaves.**

Some moth and sawfly larvae feed on sunflower leaves at night. If you see holes in your sunflower leaves, take a flashlight and check the plants at night. If you see larvae, knock them off the plant's leaves.

A moth larva on a sunflower leaf.

▼ **A child watering young sunflower plants.** By early summer, these sunflower plants have not grown as high as the child who is watering them. But by the end of summer, some of them may be fifteen or twenty feet high.

◀ **Rows of sunflowers tied to support poles.**

Sunflower plants are sometimes tied to support poles. The tall plants can become top-heavy, and occasionally will topple over. This usually only happens in poorly tilled soil where the roots cannot get a firm hold.

▶ **Sunflower leaves seen from underneath.**

The giant sunflower leaves may measure more than a foot across and almost that wide. Water is carried to all parts of the leaf by a complex network of veins.

The main function of the sunflower stem, or stalk, is to hold the leaves up to the sunlight. There may be twenty or more large leaves on each sunflower plant. The stalk must be very strong to support them all.

The plant stem also serves as a kind of transportation system. Food that is produced in the leaves is carried to other parts of the plant by tubelike veins in the stem, called vascular bundles. The sunflower stalk also transports water and nutrients absorbed from the soil by the plant's roots to other parts of the plant.

Sunflower plants grow very tall—mature plants may measure fifteen or twenty feet by the end of summer. In order to support such a tall stalk, the sunflower root system must be very well developed. Some sunflower roots may grow nine or ten feet long.

◀ **Insects found on sunflowers.**

The large sunflower leaves provide insects with shade from the hot sun and shelter from rainfall and heavy dew. The left photo shows a ladybug on a leaf; the right photo shows a moth on a leaf stem.

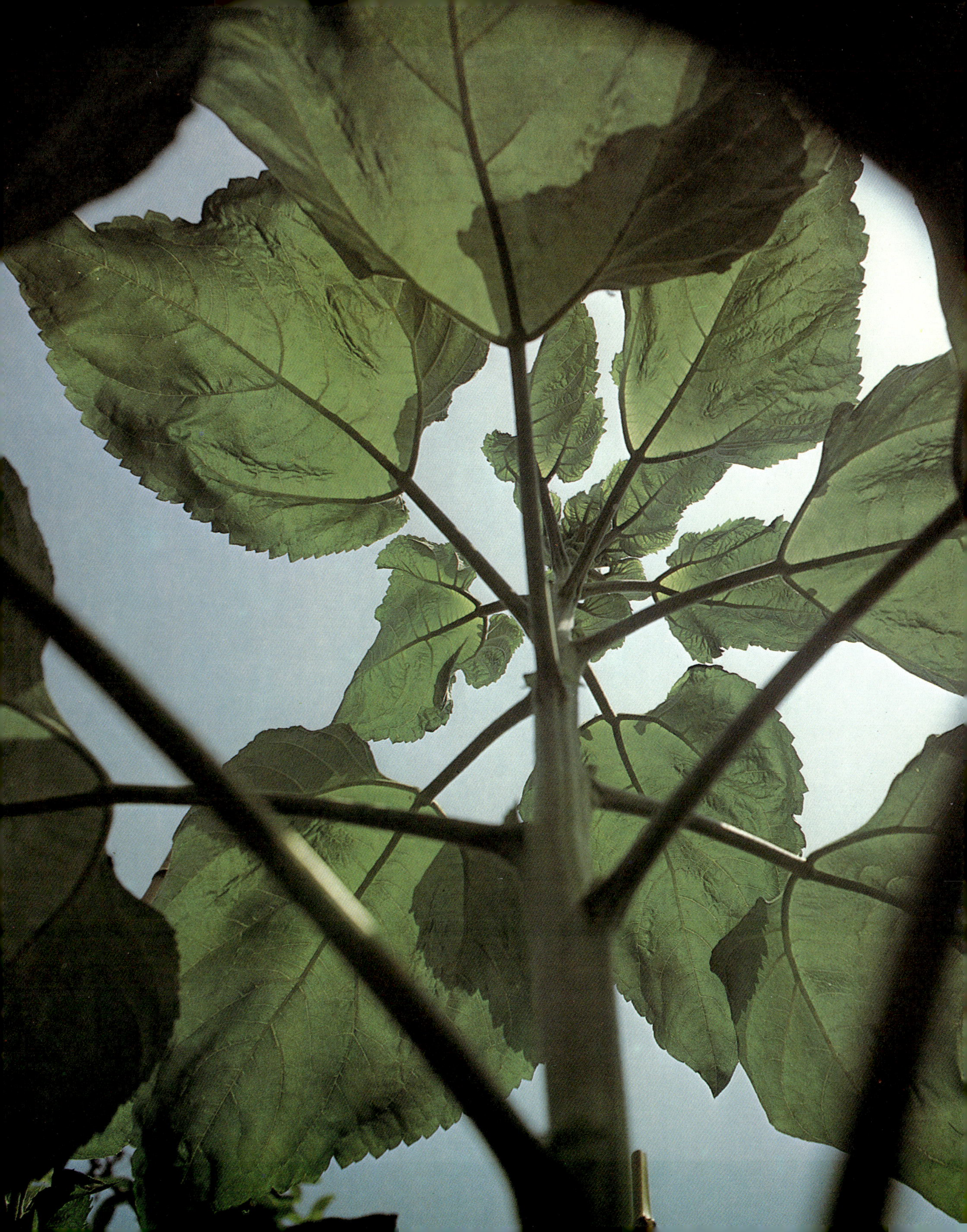

◀ **A flower bud surrounded by bracts.**

The many layers of pointed bracts protect the flower bud. They keep the bud well hidden when it is first forming.

▶ **The flower bud swells.**

As the bud grows larger and wider, the bracts unfold, and it is possible to see the flower bud.

By the time the plant has formed most of its leaves, tiny flower buds begin to appear. They form at the very top of the sunflower stalk and at the tips of some of its branches. Enclosed in each bud is a head of many tiny flowers, packed tightly together. The flower buds are enclosed by sharply pointed leaflike structures called bracts. They help to protect the developing flowers from insects and bad weather. All of the bracts together make up the involucre.

◀ **Buds of branch flowers.**

Most people think that sunflowers have just one giant flower at the top of the stalk. But smaller flowers sometimes bloom from branches, as well. In the left photo, a flower bud is forming on a branch. In the right photo, a bud begins to swell.

12

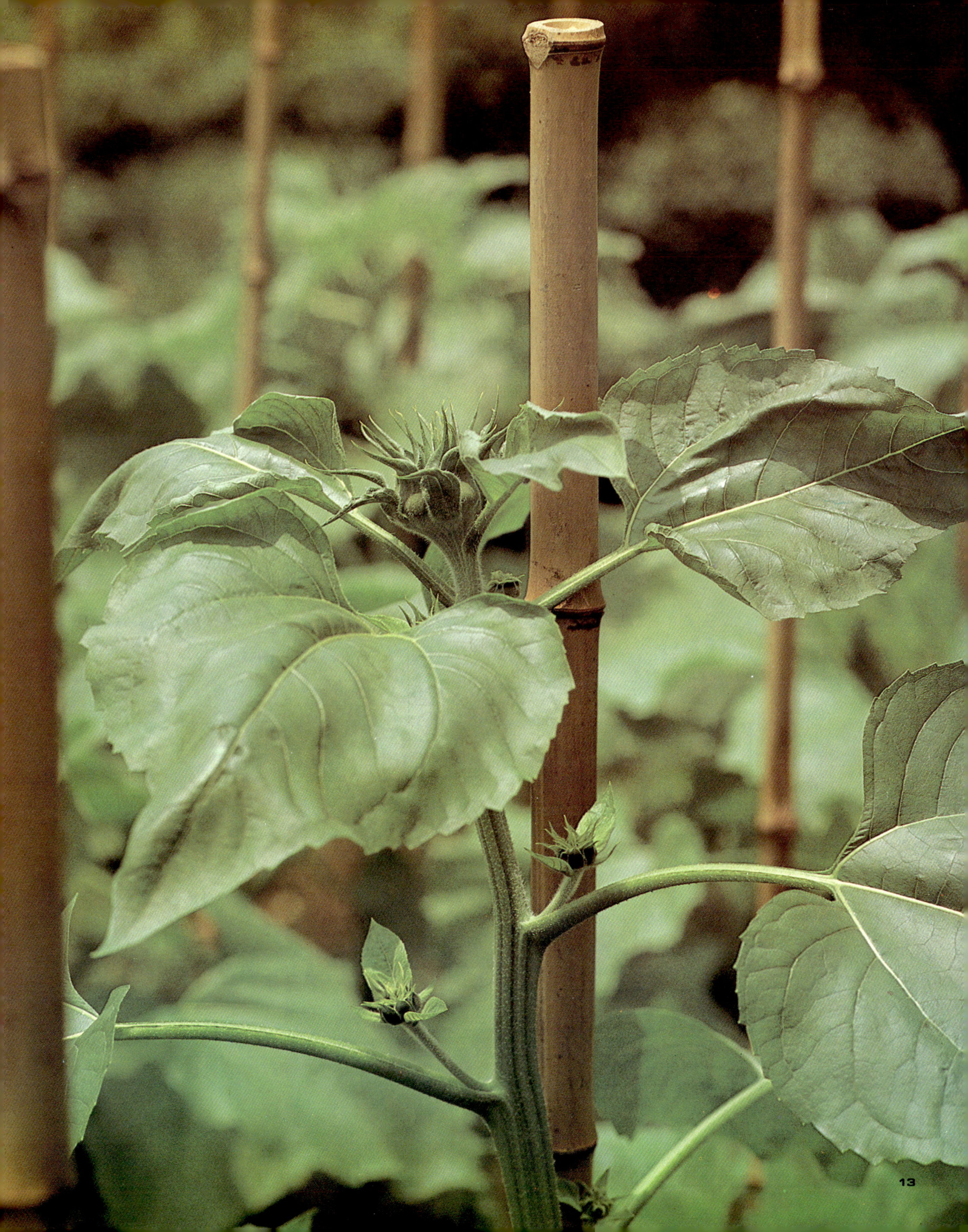

▲ **A sunflower bud covered by the involucre.**
The bracts of the involucre are covered with tiny hairs. These help to protect the buds from insects.

▲ **Cross-section of a sunflower head.**
The enlarged end of the flower stalk that holds the flowers is called the receptacle.

Flowers are very important to plants because they form the seeds from which new plants can grow. If you were to cut open a sunflower bud, you would see pale flower petals and many tiny flowers packed closely together. The plant's seeds will form from the tiny flowers.

Because sunflower plants are so very large, they need to absorb a lot of sunlight in order to produce enough food for themselves. So they actually follow the movement of the sun throughout the day. This movement toward light is called phototropism. In early morning, sunflower leaves and buds are turned toward the east, where the sun rises. As the sun makes its way west throughout the day, the plant bends in that direction. Sunflowers do this from the time they are seedlings until the flower head is completely open. Movement of the flower heads stops after they have opened. Then all the flowers face toward the east.

● **Watch sunflower plants follow the sun.**
Young sunflower plants follow the sun as it travels from east to west across the sky each day. Check your sunflower plant several times a day to see it turn with the sun.

▼ **A bud turning its head to catch the sunlight.** Sunflower buds and leaves bend in the direction of the sun to catch its light.

▲ **A bud beginning to open up.**

The involucre slowly unfolds, revealing the flowers that were hidden inside.

▲ **The petals beginning to unfurl.**

One by one the yellow petals are raised up, then opened out flat.

Sunflower plants begin to bloom when they are about three months old. Once the flower bud has reached full growth, it begins to open up. Slowly the green, pointed bracts of the involucre unfold. Then the yellow petals begin to rise, one by one. It takes several days for the flower to come into full bloom. The sunflower may measure as much as two feet across when it is completely opened up.

◀ **An involucre that has started to open before the flower bud has fully formed.**

Sometimes, especially with branch flowers, an involucre opens too soon. Then it is possible to see the flower bud developing inside.

▼ **A sunflower in full bloom.** By the third day, the petals of this sunflower have completely opened. They are bright gold, tinged with orange. Dark sunflower seeds have not yet formed in the center of the flower.

◀ **Sunflowers in bloom.**

There are about seventy kinds, or species, of sunflowers in the world. Many of them grow wild along roadsides and in fields. Others are raised for food and for sunflower oil.

▶ **Sunflowers growing in a highland field.**

The sunflower is not really a single flower at all. It is made up of many tiny, individual flowers, or florets, that are clustered together. Flowers whose heads are made up of numerous tiny flowers are called composites. Sunflowers, dandelions, daisies, and chicory all belong to the Compositae family.

The sunflower has two different kinds of flowers. The large, bright yellow petals that frame the flower head are actually individual florets, called ray florets. The tiny, tubelike flowers in the center are the disc florets. There may be more than two thousand disc florets on one sunflower head. The function of the disc florets is to produce seeds from which new plants can grow. The ray florets are not able to produce seeds.

◀ **Other types of sunflowers (photos 1-2).**

The scientific name for the small sunflower at the left is *Helianthus debilis*. The *Helianthus annuus* at the right has round double flowers.

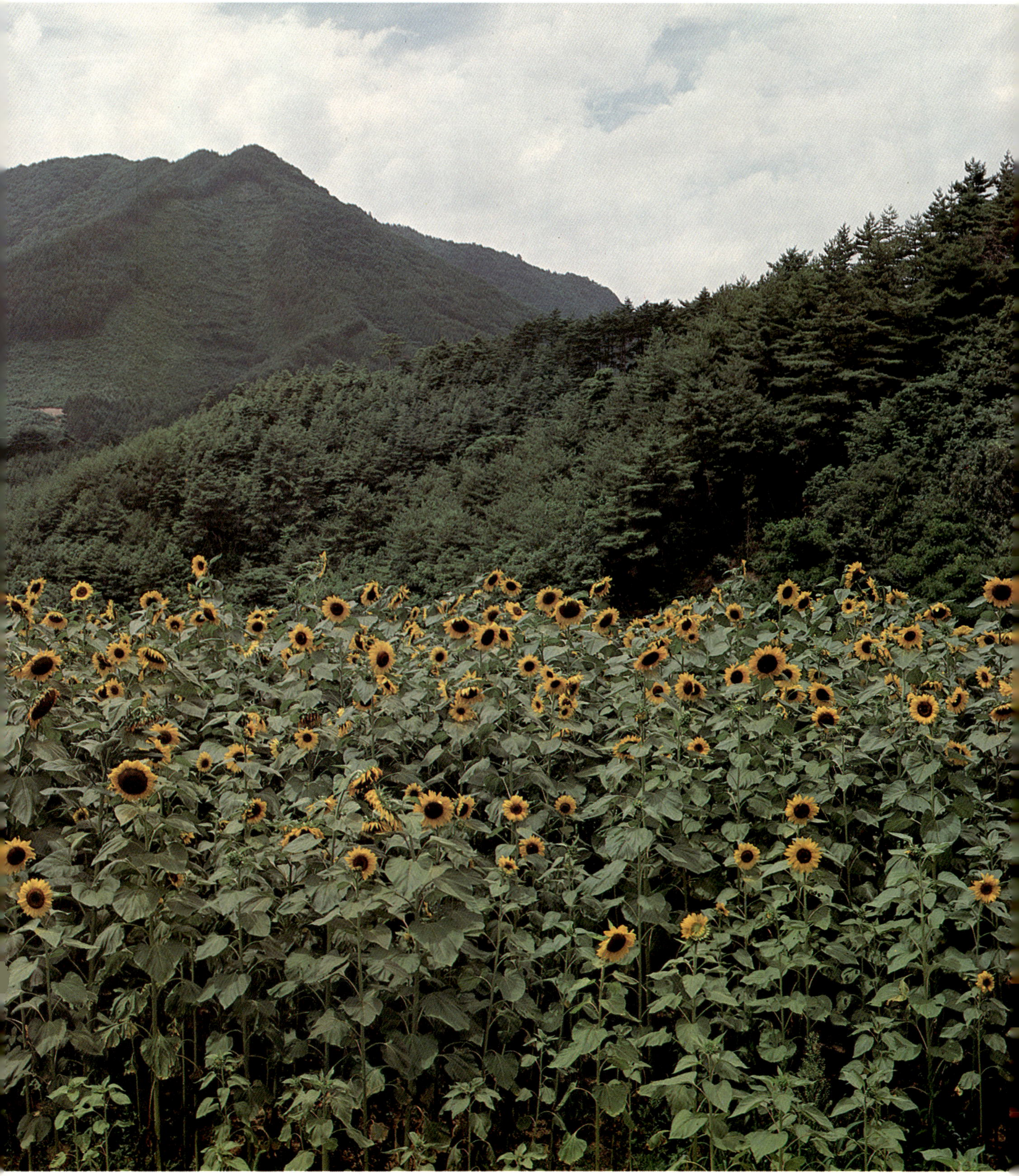

◀ **A tall sunflower in bloom.**

In a field of sunflowers, the plant in the shadiest spot will grow tallest because it must stretch furthest to catch the sun's rays.

▶ **The sunflower changes daily.**

As the disc florets bloom, the sunflower's center, or disc, darkens. It also grows larger, sometimes doubling in size. A mature disc may measure a foot wide. The weight of the flower makes it bend down toward the ground.

Once the large yellow petals have opened, the disc florets begin to flower. Those nearest the ray florets open up first. As more and more of the tiny tubelike flowers bloom, the green center of the sunflower grows smaller and smaller. When the center of the sunflower has turned dark, all of the disc florets have bloomed.

Although the ray florets cannot produce seeds, they serve another important function. Their bright yellow color attracts bees, butterflies, and other insects to the sunflower. The large petals also serve as a platform on which the insects can land.

Insects and plants have developed a helping relationship. Plants produce pollen and nectar. Both are good food for insects. As insects flit from flower to flower, searching for food, they carry pollen from one plant to another. Many plants, including many sunflowers, need pollen from another plant in order to produce seeds to start new plants. Insects helps this pollination process to take place.

● **Measuring the sunflower's size.**

When the flowers are in bloom, the sunflower stalk stops growing. All of the plant's energy is directed toward the flowers now. A mature sunflower stalk is about two inches thick at the base.

A sunflower stalk next to a bamboo pole.

4th day after coming into bloom	6th day	7th day
8th day	9th day	10th day
11th day	14th day	15th day

anthers
petals
calyx
ovary

stigma
anthers

◀ **Close-up of a sunflower.**

The disc florets in this sunflower are in various stages of blooming. Those near the outer part of the flower head (disc) have bloomed first. Those in the center will bloom last.

▶ **Cross-section of a sunflower head.**

You can see the many rows of tiny disc florets in various stages of blooming. Soon after a floret is pollinated, a seed begins to grow in the ovary. As the ovaries of the florets swell up, the flower disc grows wider.

Sunflowers reproduce in a very complex way. Although there are both male and female parts in each disc floret, they develop at different times. So sunflowers do not usually pollinate themselves. The male anthers push up from the floret first and release the pollen. Then the female stigma uncurls its tips and holds them out, ready to receive pollen from another plant.

If you look closely at the sunflower head in the photo opposite, you can see the disc florets in various stages of blooming. The outer florets, with their tiny yellow petals, have fully opened flowers. The next circle of florets has given off its pollen; the stigmas are holding out their tips, waiting to receive pollen from another plant. The next inner circle of florets shows the dark stamens, where pollen is being pushed out of the anther tubes. The stigmas of these florets are still tightly closed. The florets in the very center of the sunflower have not yet started to open up.

◀ **The parts of a disc floret.**

The female pistil is a long, thick tube with a stigma at the tip and an ovary at the base. The male stamen is actually five stamens fused together. The tips of the stamens are the anthers, which hold the yellow pollen grains. The calyx protects the bud of some flowers, but it is not important in the sunflower because it has an involucre.

The anther tube from the outside (left) and inside (right).

Pollen being pushed out of the anther tube.

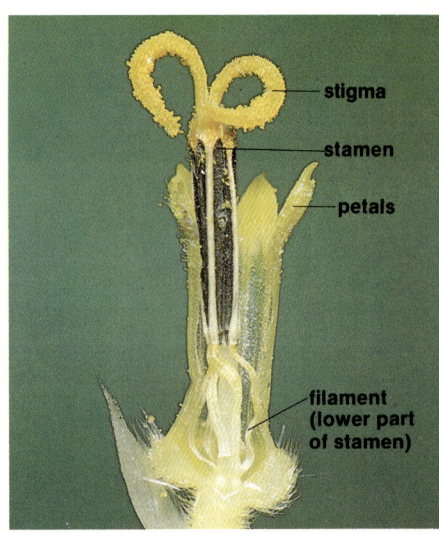

The stigma is ready to be pollinated.

If you were to look at a single disc floret very closely, you would see the parts that are shown in the photos above. The tips of the stamens, the anthers, are fused together to form the anther tube. The female pistil is enclosed in the anther tube. At the base of the pistil is the ovary, where a seed will eventually form.

As the pistil begins to push its way up through the anther tube, it brushes pollen along with it from the anthers. Finally, the pollen is pushed out through the tip of the anther tube. It is carried, by insects or the wind, to other sunflower plants. Only then does the stigma, the tip of the pistil, uncurl its two tips. It is ready to receive pollen from another sunflower plant.

But if pollination does not occur for some reason, the sunflower may pollinate itself. The stigma will form a loop and curl completely around until it touches any pollen that might be remaining on the outside of the anther tube.

● Other composite flowers.

Asters (left photo) and cosmos (right photo) also belong to the Compositae family. The photo at the far right shows both a disc floret and a ray floret of a cosmos.

▼ Insects attracted to sunflowers (photos 1-3). (1) Honeybees collecting pollen and nectar from sunflowers. (2) A small chafer beetle eating sunflower pollen. (3) A praying mantis nymph on a sunflower. Mantises hunt, or prey upon, other insects.

▼ **As summer ends, the sunflowers go to seed.** The bright yellow petals begin to wither and fade as the plant goes to seed. The leaves, too, begin to droop.

▲ The base of each disc floret helps to protect the seed developing inside.

When the pistils die, the bases of the disc florets expand and turn green. They protect the seeds from insects and keep them from drying out.

▲ A view of the sunflower seeds developing inside the involucre.

The seeds are white at first, but they gradually increase in size and turn darker. The involucre helps to protect the seeds as they mature.

Once the disc floret is pollinated, the pollen grain begins to absorb sugar and water from the stigma on which it has landed. It swells up and sends a long tube down the neck of the pistil. When it reaches the ovary, a male sperm cell from the pollen grain joins with an egg. From this fertilized egg, a seed begins to form.

As the seeds form in the ovaries of the disc flowers, the ovaries swell up, and the sunflower head grows larger and heavier. Its weight makes it bend toward the ground. The gigantic sunflower leaves begin to droop. Most of the food that is produced by the plant is now sent to the developing seeds.

▶ A young sunflower seed.

Each seed contains nutrients and the embryo from which a new plant can grow.

A seed and its cross-section.

The seed (arrow) and its shell.

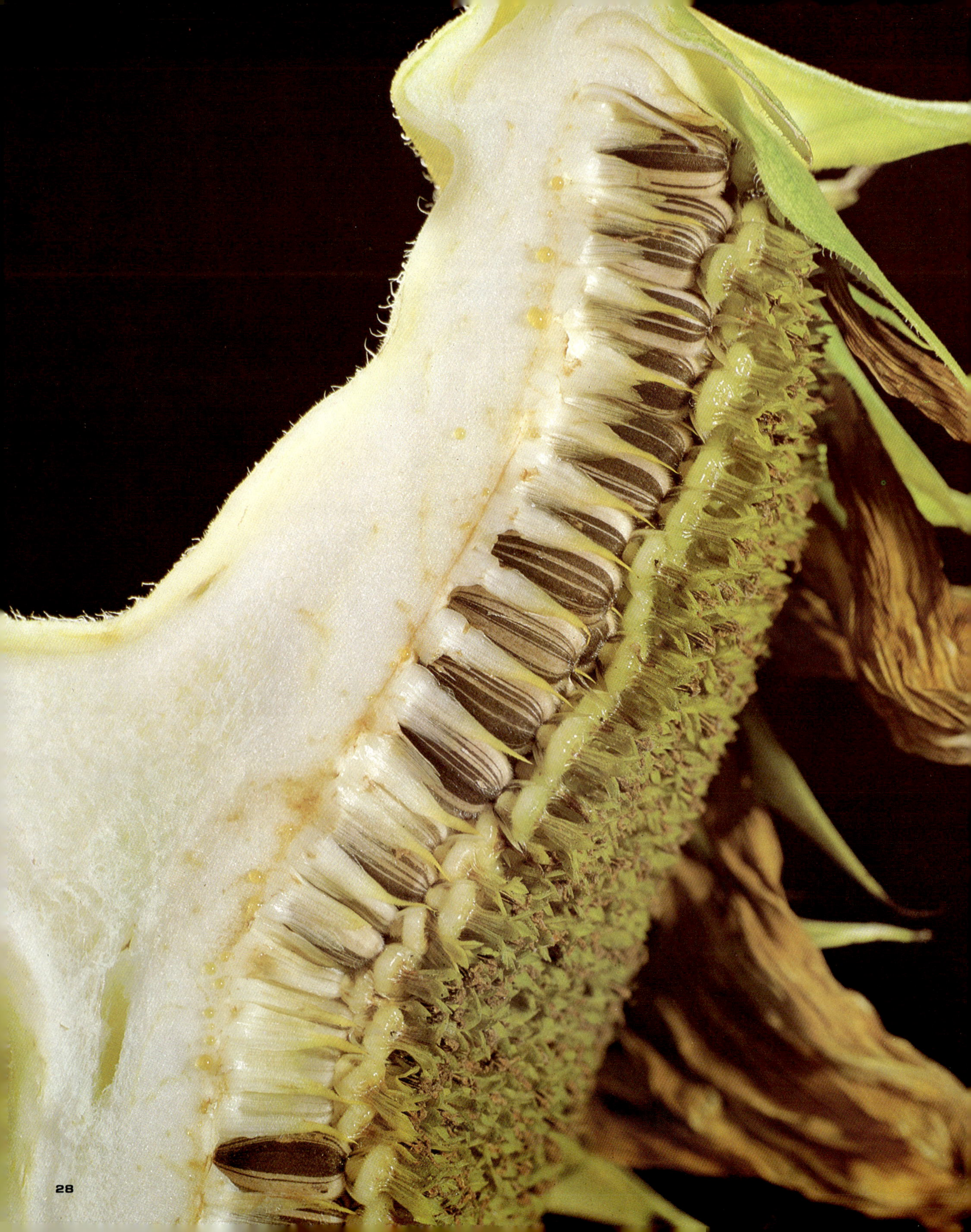

◀ **Cross-section of a sunflower head.**

Hundreds of seeds are developing on the flower disc. They are nourished by food that is carried to them by the plant stem.

▲ **Seeds in various stages of ripening.**

As the seed develops, it darkens and begins to dry out. The protective green base of the disc floret eventually falls away.

The sunflower seeds, which are small and white at first, soon grow larger and turn darker. If you were to look at a cross-section of a sunflower head in autumn, you would see hundreds of dark sunflower seeds packed together in rows.

Each seed remains enclosed in the ovary. Eventually, the ovary hardens and dries out, forming a protective shell. The dried-up fruit (ovary) that contains the sunflower seed is called an achene. When people eat sunflower seeds, they crack open the achene and eat the seed inside.

▲ **A sunflower head full of ripe seeds.**

When the disc florets fall away at a touch, the seeds are ripe and ready to be picked.

▲ **Sunflower seeds ready to fall from the disc.**

If sunflower seeds are left on the plant, birds and other animals will eat them.

▲ In autumn, the sunflower leaves and stalk die.

▲ A large root system anchored this sunflower.

In autumn, the leaves and stem of the sunflower plant begin to die. The plant's most important job—that of producing seeds from which new plants can grow—is finished. The heavy flower heads nod toward the ground, ready to drop their seeds at any moment.

Each seed contains a tiny plant embryo with nutrients stored in the seed leaves—everything that is necessary to form a new plant. Sunflower seeds that drop to the ground in autumn may begin to germinate immediately, if there is enough moisture in the ground. But they will not be able to flower during the cold winter. It is best for sunflower seeds to be planted in the spring of the year, when the conditions are right for new plants to grow.

Cross-section of a seed.

A seed that's absorbed water.

◀ A seed ready to germinate.

If a seed is soaked overnight, it will absorb water. As it swells up, the seed coat splits. A tiny structure appears. The lower part, called the hypocotyl, will form the root. The upper part, the epicotyl, will carry the seed leaves out of the soil. The seed leaves are called cotyledons.

▼ **Sunflower seeds produced by one sunflower.** More than 1,500 seeds were produced by this single sunflower.

GLOSSARY

achene—a dried fruit which contains a single seed. (p. 29)

bracts—the pointed, leaflike structures that protect the flower bud of the sunflower. All of the bracts together make up the involucre. (p. 12)

composite—many small flowers clustered together, which look like a single large flower. (p. 18)

cotyledons—seed leaves, the first leaves to form on a plant. They contain stored nutrients. (p. 30)

embryo—the early stages of development of a plant or other organism. (p. 30)

floret—a tiny flower, usually one of many in a flower head. Disc florets are those in the center of composite flowers. Ray florets are those found at the outer edge of composite flowers. (pp. 18, 20)

photosynthesis—the complex process by which green plants make food, with the help of chlorophyll, a substance found in the plants' leaves, and energy from sunlight. (p. 8)

phototropism—movement toward light. (p. 14)

pollination—the process in which pollen is transferred from an anther to the tip, or stigma, of a pistil. (pp. 20, 24)

vascular bundles—tubelike veins in a plant stem or leaf in which food and water are carried from one part of the plant to another. (p. 10)

Sunflowers /
J 583.55 P
Pohl, Kathleen.
PORTAGE PUBLIC LIB   09838

318148500069581

J583.55   Pohl, Kathleen
   P   Sunflowers

Por. 10/95

Portage Public Library

PORTAGE